A B C D E

F G H I J K

L M N O P

Q R S T U

V W X Y Z

ISBN-13: 978-1536820096
ISBN-10: 1536820091
Story by Barbara Miller
Illustrations by Martina Cecilia
Book Design by Adrian Navarrete

Lily Lemon Blossom

Story by Barbara Miller
Illustrations by Martina Cecilia

A-B-C are painting
a smiley face on the
sun in the sky.

D-E-F-G are dusting
the sleepy clouds as
they pass by.

H-I-J-K are busy
sprinkling raindrops on
the flowers below.

LMNO

While twinkling lights are
placed on the moon,
by L-M-N and O.

Oh dear, someone is missing! Where are P-Q-R-S and T?

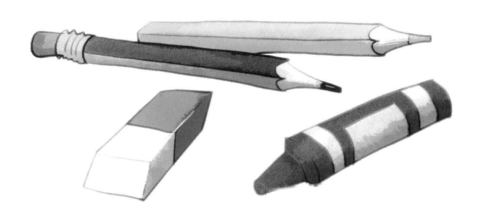

Oh, here they are! Painting the rainbow. Isn't it pretty?!

U and V are showing the
bluebirds how to twirl in
the breeze. They even
help the baby birds settle
gently into the trees.

W-X-Y-Z are
collecting and
returning the
fallen stars.

I'll bet you didn't know the alphabets were so important. Well they really, really are.

The End

A B C D E

F G H I J K

L M N O P

Q R S T U

V W X Y Z

Lily Lemon Blossom
Children's Picture Books

Lily Lemon Blossom

TRICK OR TREAT ON BLOSSOM'S STREET

Story by Barbara Miller
Illustrations by Martina Cecilia

Lily Lemon Blossom

A Very Lily Christmas

Story by Barbara Miller
Illustrations by Martina Cecilia

Ages 3-6

Lily Lemon Blossom

Numbers

Lily's 123

Story by Barbara Miller
Illustrations by Martina Cecilia

Let's count together from 1 to 10!

Ages 3-6

Lily Lemon Blossom

Lily's ABC

ABC SHOW AND TELL

Alphabet

Story by Barbara Miller
Illustrations by Martina Cecilia

Learning the ABC's has never been so much fun!

Collect Them All

Made in the USA
Lexington, KY
12 September 2016